For Every Dog An Angel

written and illustrated by
Christine Davis

For Every Dog An Angel

© Copyright 2004 by Christine Davis

Printed in Hong Kong

Lighthearted Press Inc.
P.O. Box 90125
Portland, OR 97290

ISBN 0-9659225-2-9

10 9 8 7 6 5 4 3 2

From the author.....

In 1995 I unexpectedly lost my beloved dog, Martha... my forever dog.
She and I had shared many adventures over thirteen years and I thought
there would be many more yet to come. I felt I had fallen off the
wondrous path Martha and I had been traveling together. "But Chris,"
a wise friend said to me, "this IS your path – it just doesn't look the
way you thought it would look."

I began searching for a way to thank Martha for the magic she had
brought into my life. I knew the bond we had shared was so strong
it would keep us connected through time and space. The story of
FOR EVERY DOG AN ANGEL was sent down from the heavens, through the
starry skies, into my hopeful heart. I heard the words and found peace
in knowing Martha was happy and whole again, watching over me as
I continued along on my journey without her by my side.

One of the special gifts of this book has been connecting with animal
lovers all over the world. I would like to thank all the people who have
taken the time to share their stories with me about their own magical
dogs. For all of you who have found your forever dogs.... and for those
still hoping to.... I offer this little book.

With love and gratitude,
Chris Davis

For Martha,
my forever dog,
whose
gentle spirit
and
magic heart
light the pages
of this book.

Whenever a puppy is born on earth
a guardian angel waits nearby
to welcome the puppy into the world
and take it under her heavenly wings.

The
guardian
angel makes
herself very
small and snuggles in close to the soft,
warm fur, telling her puppy how much it is loved
and that it has come into the world
for a special purpose. Even though the
puppy's eyes are closed, it feels the
fluttering wings by its heart and
knows its guardian angel
is there.

All puppies come into the world with unique gifts. As time passes and the puppy grows, the guardian angel helps her puppy to understand what makes it so very special. Whether they are destined to become

fast runners,

soulful singers

or

peaceful sleepers,

each puppy is perfect and the angel loves it just the way it is.

The day comes when the puppy must go into the world and start traveling down its own special path.

Sometimes that path leads to a special place, where a family has been waiting for their puppy to find them. And the guardian angel is happy, knowing her dog has found a loving home and it will never...

ever...

be left behind.

Angels like to visit when their dogs are dreaming. You may have seen a dog's paws moving while it is asleep. Perhaps it is on a high hill in a faraway place, dancing with its guardian angel.

All dogs bring the gift of love to the world. In that way they are very much like angels. Dogs will share their love with anyone. They don't ask for anything in return. But if someone takes a moment to scratch a dog under its chin and tell a dog how special it is, you can be sure its guardian angel is smiling.

From time to time, when a certain person and a certain dog meet, something happens that is just like magic!

It is as if they have known each other before.

Each knows what the other is thinking and feeling.

They will be together always. And the guardian angel watches over the two with love, knowing her dog has found its forever person and the person has found their forever dog.

A forever person and their forever dog will share many experiences over a lifetime like listening to favorite stories

and visiting friends who need cheering up.

HOSPITAL

Animal Therapist Visiting Today

They will watch hundreds of sunsets from up on the hill.

But the greatest gift these two will share is knowing what is in the other's heart. Side by side, looking up at the sky on a starry night, a forever person and their forever dog will share all the secret hopes and dreams that are only told to a very best friend.

A dog can never really be separated from its forever person. Neither time nor space can ever come between them. So when the dog comes to the end of its earthly life and must go on ahead without its person beside them, the guardian angel becomes a loving bridge that connects the two friends for as long as the person remains on earth.

Sometimes dogs will cross the angel bridge
and visit the earth while they are waiting
for their forever person to join them.
You can never be certain
where they might
turn up.

You may feel four paws padding along next to you when you are walking in the park.

isten carefully and you might hear
a familiar voice joining in when you go holiday caroling.

So if you see the blanket rumple softly after you've curled up for an afternoon nap, it's very possible your forever dog has come back to visit and is napping beside you.

Nothing brings your forever dog more joy
      than knowing you are happy, even if that means
   bringing a new dog companion into your life.
     Your forever dog lovingly
   remembers the special place
it had in your heart,
and is delighted to know
another dog will get to
share all the love
you have to
   offer.

Animal Shelter

Your forever dog may even come back and show your new dog the best spots for burying bones and where to watch for your return at the end of the day.

So don't be surprised to see your new dog racing through the house as if it's playing with an invisible friend... it probably is.

As the years go by you and your dog may find yourselves going more slowly as you take your daily walks. The time may come when your dog leaves your side and crosses the bridge to be with your forever dog. In fact, there may be many animals who will share your life during the time you are here on earth.

One day,
the angel bridge
that your
forever dog crossed
so many years earlier
will appear to you.
And with the happy heart
of a person who is going home,
you will cross the bridge
and find yourself welcomed
by all the animal friends
you made when you
were on earth.

In the middle of all that love your forever dog will be waiting for you. It will be like the day you found each other on earth. You will know you have been together before, and nothing will ever separate you again.

And the angels will be happy,
knowing a forever person and their forever dog ☆
have found each other once more.

We hope you enjoyed this
Lighthearted Press book. To order additional copies
please call our toll-free order number
1-87PETLOVER (1-877-385-6837) or send
$9.95 per copy plus $4.00 shipping per order to:

Lighthearted Press Inc.
P.O. Box 90125 · Portland, Oregon 97290
503-786-3085 (Phone)
503-786-0315 (Fax)
1-87PETLOVER (Toll-free)
davis@lightheartedpress.com
www.lightheartedpress.com

Also by Christine Davis
FOR EVERY CAT AN ANGEL